$13.54

P9-BZC-844

R VG

OBSOLETE

I Look
like a Girl

I Look like a Girl

Sheila Hamanaka

MORROW JUNIOR BOOKS
New York

Oil paints were used for the full-color illustrations.
The text type is 28-point Opti Adrift.

Published by Morrow Junior Books
a division of William Morrow and Company, Inc.
1350 Avenue of the Americas, New York, NY 10019
www.williammorrow.com

Printed in Hong Kong by South China Printing Company (1988) Ltd.

10   9   8   7   6   5   4   3   2   1

Library of Congress Cataloging-in-Publication Data
Hamanaka, Sheila.
I look like a girl/Sheila Hamanaka.
p. cm.
Summary: In her imagination, a young girl assumes many shapes
and forms, from dolphin and condor to wolf and jaguar.
ISBN 0-688-14625-2 (trade)—ISBN 0-688-14626-0 (library)
[1. Imagination—Fiction.   2. Animals—Fiction.   3. Stories in rhyme.]
I. Title.   PZ8.3.H17I1 1999   [E]—dc21   98-44723   CIP AC

TO THREE
GENERATIONS
OF TIGERS:

In loving memory of
Dorothy Briley,
who made possible
the creation of the book
ON THE WINGS OF PEACE

In support of Julia Butterfly
and her world's longest tree-sit
in defense of the ancient
redwood named Luna

And in celebration of
Sachiko "Sachi-cub"
Pease Davis,
my first grandchild
and tiger cub

I look like a girl,

but I'm really a tiger,
with a rumble, a roar, and a leap!

I look like a girl,

but I'm really a dolphin,

with a
spin and a splash
in the sea.